ORCHIDS AND MISTLETOE

A SECRETS AND SPIES SERIES NOVELLA

KATE BATEMAN

K. C. BATEMAN

CHAPTER 1

eptford docks, London. December 1816.

DEATHBED PROMISES WERE THE *WORST*.

Christopher 'Kit' Carlisle tightened his fingers around the silver locket in his hand. The trinket, with its delicate scrolls and tiny ferns, had been the only thing of beauty in his filthy prison cell. The chain was long gone, used as a bribe for one of the guards, but Kit would guard the locket with his life, just as he'd promised.

His old friend's last plea echoed in his ears.

"Give this to m'sister." Andrew's voice had been scarcely more than a whisper as he'd pressed the locket into Kit's hand with the last glimmer of his strength. He'd kept it hidden for their entire incarceration, a reminder of another, happier life.

"Take care of her for me, won't you? Tell her what happened?"

"I will. I swear."

They'd both known Andrew wouldn't live to complete the task himself. He'd succumbed to his wounds the following night, slipping away from the squalor of the cell where they'd both been held as prisoners of war, courtesy of Bonaparte.

Kit shook his head, dislodging the painful memory. That had been almost eighteen months ago, and unlike Andrew, he'd survived. Raven, his friend and fellow agent, better known to the *ton* as Lord William Ravenwood, had pulled off a daring rescue just as Kit himself had been knocking at death's door.

His recovery had taken months. He'd lost so much weight he'd looked like a walking skeleton, and he'd been haunted by memories of his imprisonment, racked with guilt that he'd survived to return to England while Andrew had been buried in a dusty, unmarked grave in Northern Spain.

Kit swallowed down a ball of gratitude for his brothers-in-arms. Raven, Nic, and Richard had refused to let him retreat into darkness and self-pity. They'd employed a relentless combination of bullying and kindness to help him recover.

Nic—ever the Frenchman—had engaged one of the best chefs in London to create delicious meals to tempt his appetite. Richard had trained with him daily. First with gentle exercises, and then with more strenuous fencing and boxing, tirelessly repeating the same moves over and over to rebuild his wasted muscles. Raven had regaled him with a constant stream of gossip, keeping him abreast of all that was happening in society, even while they were holed up in the splendid isolation of Kit's country estate, Ashford Court, near Bath.

The carriage gave a sudden jolt and Kit blinked at the hustle and bustle of London's Deptford dockyards beyond the window. His reflection stared back at him; he barely recognized himself now that he was well again. His skin had lost its unnatural pallor. He was tanned and healthy, stronger than ever, and ready—albeit reluctantly—to rejoin polite society.

Today's errand was the final step in his rehabilitation. He'd been physically capable of keeping his promise to Andrew six months ago, but the woman for whom this locket was intended, Andrew's sister, hadn't been in the country.

Lady Emma Townsend. Kit hadn't seen her for over three years, but she'd never been far from his thoughts.

She'd finally returned from her most recent expedition to South America. Her ship—not merely the vessel she'd sailed in on, but hers in the literal sense that she owned the thing outright—had docked here, at Deptford, last night.

Hence Kit's presence this morning. He would find Emma, give her the locket, and leave, free of the burden of responsibility that had plagued him for the past year and a half.

The sight of the ships beyond the carriage window caused a familiar, yet unexpected yearning in his chest. A yearning for adventure, for new horizons. After the horrors of Spain he'd never thought he'd want to leave England again, but perhaps the return of his urge to travel wasn't so strange. He'd been stuck inside for the first six months of his convalescence, after all, and for the past year he'd barely seen anyone save his three friends and their wives.

It was definitely time to rejoin the world.

A flurry of sleet swirled past the window and Kit took a deep breath, relishing the crisp bite of cold air in his lungs, so different from the dry, dusty heat of Spain. It was less than a week until Christmas. He disliked crowds, but he would force himself to attend a few of the endless parties here in town, and then he could retreat to Ashford Court and relish the peace and solitude once more.

But first, the locket. And Emma.

His stomach knotted in mingled anticipation and dread of seeing her again. He'd changed so much from the boy she'd once known. Would she even recognize him after all this time?

CHAPTER 2

"*D*on't you dare die on me!"

Emma Townsend thrust an accusing finger at the wilting orchid in front of her.

The plant—unsurprisingly—made no response.

"I did *not* spend countless hours coddling you across the Atlantic to have you give up the ghost as soon as we reached England," she scolded. "Now buck up."

Her spirits, already low, ebbed some more. She'd had such high hopes when she'd left Brazil, but so few of her precious specimens had survived. Captain Horner had kindly allowed her to use the chart room to house her plants, since it received the most light, but the poor things were still flagging badly.

The view from the mullioned bay window was equally depressing. London looked much as she recalled. Cold, grey, bleak. A watery sun filtered weakly through clouds and the air smelled foul, of refuse and coal. Sailors, dock workers, and tarts hustled about their business, dodging cranes and winches unloading crates of produce. Mudlarks, mostly young children dressed in rags, scoured the water's edge searching for anything they could sell.

Emma shivered. She'd forgotten this damp chill; such a contrast to the humid heat of the rainforest. She'd give anything to be off again, setting sail for somewhere warm and colorful, but it would be weeks before she could do such a thing. She *would* go —just as soon as she'd honored Andrew by getting these blasted orchids named after him.

If any of the bloody things survived this infernal cold.

She was certain the plants in front of her were a new species of orchid, an as-yet-unclassified sub-species of *oncidium*. All she had to do was keep one of the pathetic-looking things alive, and flowering, to present to the gentlemen of the Botanical Society at their next meeting in two weeks' time. But of the twenty three specimens she'd brought from Rio de Janeiro, eighteen had already perished. Only five appeared to be clinging to life.

Emma kicked a nearby wooden packing crate in frustration. "Blasted things. Why must you be so contrary?"

She would be glad to get off this accursed boat and on to dry land.

* * *

"I'M NO EXPERT, but I don't think talking to them has any effect."

Emma yelped. The gruff voice, rich with amusement, had come from directly behind her. She spun around in alarm, her hand pressed to her throat, and stumbled back into a crate.

The intruder filled the shadowed stairway that led down from the upper deck. His shoulders—made even broader by a dark woolen greatcoat—blocked out almost all the light from above. Her heart hammered at his imposing size, but she tilted her chin in challenge.

"This is a private cabin, sir," she managed coolly.

"I apologize. I was looking for Lady Emma Townsend."

Emma frowned. The giant must be a dockhand who'd been directed to help her unload her plants.

"I am she."

She dragged her eyes from his impressive physique and gestured to the nearest crate. "Please be careful with those particular plants. They're extremely fragile. A carriage should be waiting for me on the dockside—they need to be placed in there so I can personally see them to my London residence."

The stranger stepped into the light, and Emma's breath caught.

"Kit?" she gasped.

The corner of his mouth turned up in a wry smile at her stunned disbelief. "In the flesh."

Dear God in Heaven, it *was* him!

The one man she hadn't expected.

The one man she'd secretly longed to see.

"You're back," she stammered, amazed and slightly disoriented by his sudden appearance. "In London, I mean."

"As are you. Did you have a successful trip?"

"Er. Yes. Indeed."

Her heart began to pound in earnest and heat crept into her cheeks. Her brother's friend was still, unquestionably, the most striking man she'd ever seen. Handsome was too soft a word for the harsh angularity of his face. His nose had a slight bump near the bridge, as if it had been broken a time or two, and a slim scar that hadn't been there three years ago bisected the edge of one tawny eyebrow. Neither 'flaw' detracted from his attractiveness in the slightest.

His piercing gray eyes were still the same, as were the lips she'd fantasized about kissing ever since she'd been a girl of sixteen. He was both achingly familiar . . . and subtly different. Older, broader. *Wilder.*

Flustered, Emma quelled the bizarre impulse to simply throw herself into his arms.

She hadn't seen the man for years, for heaven's sake. He probably still thought of her as Andrew's annoying little sister.

He was staring at her expectantly, and while there were a thousand things she wanted to say to him, a thousand questions she wanted to ask, her tongue seemed to have tied itself into knots.

"I . . . need some air," she stammered.

He opened his mouth to reply, but she rushed forward and he stepped aside to let her pass. She'd just put her foot on the first stair when a loud crash and a bellow of warning sounded directly above.

Kit lunged forward, shoving her back against the wall, flattening his body against hers as a huge wooden crate tumbled through the open hatchway. It crashed down the stairs behind them with a terrifying splintering of wood, missing his shoulder by barely an inch.

Emma let out a strangled yelp.

"It's all right. I've got you." Kit's deep voice rumbled in her ear.

She managed to nod, humiliatingly aware of the whole-body tingles his sudden closeness was producing. His arms had come up to bracket her head in an instinctively protective gesture and her face was squashed against his rock-hard chest. The incredible heat of his body burned through the layers of their clothes.

She told herself it was hard to breathe because she was finally wearing a corset again after weeks of going without—and not because she was in Kit's arms.

When she finally managed to inhale, she got a lungful of *him*, an unexpectedly delicious scent of male skin and cedar-based cologne. Her head swam. He might be dressed like a ruffian, but he didn't smell like one. He smelled clean and altogether too inviting.

Her cheek brushed his as she lifted her head. He pulled back— just a fraction—bringing those beautiful lips of his dangerously close to her own, and her stomach somersaulted again as he gazed down at her. The shouts and footsteps from above faded away. They were the only two people in the world.

"Thank you," Emma managed breathlessly. "I think you just saved my life."

His gaze dropped to her lips, as if anticipating a reward of the wickedest kind, and she sucked in a breath, more than willing to comply. She lifted her chin in silent invitation, but to her intense disappointment he pushed away from the wall and stepped back, releasing her.

"Think nothing of it," he growled.

Damn it. Her attraction for him had always been one-sided.

To cover her mortification she bustled over to inspect her plants, morbidly certain they'd been flattened by the wayward crate, but they were all still safe on the sill.

"All right below?" The concerned shout echoed down through the hatchway.

"Yes, thank you, Captain Horner," Emma shouted back.

Suddenly keen to escape the confines of the cabin and Kit's unnerving presence, she picked up the nearest orchid and thrust it toward him. He accepted it automatically, and she picked up one of her own, cradling the terracotta pot in front of her like a talisman to ward him off.

He glanced down at the tangle of roots and soil. "Looks dead."

She clutched her own pot protectively to her chest. "It is no such thing. It's an orchid in its dormant phase. It's supposed to look like that." She pointed at a lumpy protrusion sprouting from one of the taller shoots. "There. You see those buds? In a week or so those will produce the most beautiful purple flowers you've ever seen."

Kit shrugged and she reminded herself to stop looking at his shoulders. He was even broader than he had been, more muscular than most male members of the *ton*. More muscular than anyone, really.

"If you say so."

"I do." Emma sent him her sternest look, the one she'd perfected through years of having men doubt her expertise. It was the same look she would give the learned gentlemen of the Botanical Society if they disagreed with her contention that these plants were a previously undocumented species.

Still, that was a problem for another day. She had to have a live, flowering plant to show them first. The thought prodded her into action.

"This way." She gathered up a second pot, picked her way across the splintered ruins on the floor and ascended the stairs. Kit followed her without comment.

A smart black carriage was waiting for her on the dockside, as she'd requested, so she made her way down the gangplank and slid the plants onto the floor, between the seats. Kit deposited his own plant next to hers and she sent him what she hoped was a winning smile.

"Would you mind getting the other two orchids, please?"

"Not at all."

He disappeared back up the gangplank and Emma bit her lip. She shouldn't be asking him—*Lord Ashford*—to fetch and carry for her, but seeing him again after all this time had muddled her brain.

He'd always had this effect on her. She'd spent most of her life around men, from burly sailors to eager suitors, but never had one affected her as strongly as Kit Carlisle. He'd bewitched her, long ago, and the enchantment had never worn off.

She stepped up into the carriage, settled herself on the seat, and took a deep, calming breath.

She'd hoped that three years away from him would have made her immune to his charms, but it seemed her attraction was as strong as ever. That was going to make the next phase of her plan more awkward, but there was nothing she could do about that. Her plants were her top priority; she would do what needed to be done and ignore her own embarrassing response to the man.

In truth, his appearance here, now, was incredibly convenient. She'd meant to call on him in Somerset—albeit at a time of her own choosing, when she would have had time to prepare. Still, she would seize this unexpected opportunity.

Kit was her orchids' last hope. Or rather, his hothouse was. His country home, Ashford Court, was famous in horticultural circles for its unusual greenhouse, heated entirely by naturally-occurring geothermal springs. It would be the best possible place for her orchids to bloom.

She would make him an offer he couldn't refuse.

When he reappeared with the two remaining plants nestled in his arms she sent him a grateful smile as he deposited them at her feet in the carriage.

"Thank you."

He nodded, and she opened the door of the carriage wider. "Won't you come in here for a minute? There's something I wish to discuss."

CHAPTER 3

*K*it stared up at Emma's eager expression and tried to hide his own sense of bemusement. She'd always been attractive, but nothing could have prepared him for the full-blown ravishing beauty she'd blossomed into during their time apart. Admittedly, he hadn't been much in female company for the past year or so, but it was hard not to stare like a simpleton.

In his cell he'd often imagined a perfect woman there beside him, as a distraction. Lady Emma Townsend was better than any fantasy girl he'd ever dreamed up. Her smooth skin was touched with an unfashionable hint of sun, and when they'd been chest-to-chest her lips had been so close that he could have dipped his head and tasted her.

He'd been so tempted.

When he'd heard the snap of the crane above them he'd reacted instinctively, throwing his body against hers. At any other time his heart would have been hammering because of the near-miss or because he disliked the oppressive feeling of being belowdecks. Such small, enclosed spaces reminded him of his imprisonment. But his elevated pulse and tight chest had been for an entirely different reason—*her.*

Everything had come sharply into focus. Her green eyes, wide with alarm, the delicious press of her breasts against his chest. The light, floral fragrance of her perfume.

His cock twitched in his breeches.

For the first time in eighteen months, he felt fully awake, alive in every part of his body. It was as if he'd been half-asleep and was only now waking up.

Because of her.

With a grunt, he stepped up into the carriage.

* * *

Emma sat back against the velvet seat as Kit settled opposite her. His large body dominated the small space.

"Do you often spend your time at Deptford docks masquerading as a porter, Lord Ashford?" she asked lightly.

His lips twitched at her teasing tone. "I wasn't masquerading as anything. You're the one who made the assumption. And please, call me Kit. I think saving you from certain peril means we can skip the formalities."

Heat scalded her cheeks at the reminder of her body pressed to his, at how close his lips had been to hers.

He leaned forward and reached into the pocket of his greatcoat, and his expression sobered. "Actually, I came to find you. I need to give you this."

Emma glanced down at the object in his palm and her heart clenched in anguish as she recognized the small silver locket.

"Oh! That was mine! I gave it to Andrew when he left for war."

Tears pricked her eyes. Seeing it again was like a punch to the gut.

Kit nodded. "I know. The two of us were held in the same

prison cell for the last six months of his life." His voice was low, full of compassion. "I was with him when he died. He wanted you to have it. He asked me to give it to you."

Emma swallowed hard, determined not to cry. "Thank you." She managed a watery smile. "Forgive me. I know he's gone but this makes it . . . more *real* somehow. I've been pretending that he's simply sailing around the world, having adventures, like myself. It's hard to accept that he really is dead."

Kit's strong fingers gave hers a comforting squeeze as he closed her fist around the treasure.

"I'm sorry. I didn't wish to cause you pain. I did everything in my power to save him, but he was simply too ill. If it's any consolation, he didn't suffer for long. He slipped away not long after he tasked me with returning that to you."

The roughness of his voice revealed his own pain and regret, and Emma sent him a commiserating glance. "I'm sorry you had to deal with that. I'm glad he had someone with him, for comfort, at the end."

Kit nodded, then cleared his own throat and leaned back in his seat. The carriage rocked on its springs.

"So. My promise is kept." He reached for the door handle. "I'll bid you goodbye, Lady Emma."

Emma caught his forearm. "No, wait! Please. I . . . have a proposition for you."

His brows lifted, but she couldn't tell if it was in interest or surprise. "Go on."

She had to seize the moment. The sudden reappearance of the locket was a sign, a reminder of just how important it was to honor Andrew's memory.

"I need heat. Immediately."

Kit's lips twitched in the hint of a roguish smile.

"I mean," Emma blustered, certain he was about to misconstrue her words with a meaning far more scandalous than she'd intended. "I need a *hothouse*."

She thought she heard him mutter "disappointing" under his breath, but she couldn't be sure.

He sat back. "Forgive me for being blunt," he said, more clearly, "but you're an heiress. If you want a hothouse, why not just build one?"

"I don't have time. I need it now, this week, to ensure my orchids bloom in time to present them at the Botanical Society's meeting on the first week of January." She sent him her most winning smile. "I've heard great things about Ashford Court's hothouse."

His eyes narrowed as he seemed to sense what was coming. She paused, wondering how much to offer, then decided to go in strong.

"I'll give you five hundred pounds if you'll let me put my plants in your greenhouse for the next ten days."

His brows rose, and she prayed it was because he was impressed and not offended.

"Only ten days," she said hastily.

"Over Christmas," he growled. "It's almost Christmas Eve."

"Well, yes. I regret that the timing isn't ideal. But if you have guests coming, I promise to stay out of your way. You'll barely even know I'm there."

His brows drew down. "I do not have guests coming. I like my solitude."

"A thousand pounds," she said desperately. "Please. For Andrew. I want to name these new orchids after him." Her eyes pleaded with him to understand. "I know he's gone, but . . I just think that if I do this, then a part of him will live on. Those beautiful things will bear his name, and every time someone says it in the future they'll give him back a little bit of life."

* * *

Kit frowned. Damn it, what a ridiculous offer! The last thing he wanted was this beautiful distraction invading his home and interrupting the week of festive brooding and drinking he had planned.

Still, how could he refuse? His estates, while still profitable, had suffered from his absence and inattention for the past two years. A thousand pounds would go a long way toward setting things back on an even keel. And he *had* promised he'd try to be more sociable . . .

She was still staring up at him expectantly.

"The Ancient Greeks believed something similar," he conceded finally. "That a man could gain immortality by having his name spoken aloud by future generations. The ancient Egyptians said that *to speak the name of the dead is to make him live again.*"

She beamed, apparently warmed by the fact that he understood. "Exactly!"

He sighed. "Oh, very well. I leave for Ashford Court in the morning. Come whenever you like. But I warn you, I keep a skeleton staff, and I've given most of them the week off to be with their families. It will not be the luxury you're accustomed to."

She laughed, and the sound warmed his soul. He scowled, just to prove she didn't affect him in the slightest.

"I've just spent six months traipsing through the jungles of Brazil and another six weeks crossing the Atlantic," she said airily. "I can live without luxury, believe me. And the sooner the better, for my plants. I'll join you at Ashford Court tomorrow."

She sent him another brilliant smile and Kit suppressed a groan. *Not notice she was there?* He'd have to be dead not to notice her. Dear God, what had he let himself in for?

CHAPTER 4

*E*mma's journey to Somerset went smoothly enough, despite the usual pre-Christmas delays. As her carriage finally swept along the drive that led to Ashford Court she tried not to be impressed—and failed. Andrew had described it to her several times, but her imagination hadn't done the place justice. There was something particularly welcoming about the mellow stone façade and landscaped parkland, even with the slight dusting of snow that covered the ground.

She'd hoped Kit himself might welcome her, but a polite, elderly housekeeper showed her to her room instead. Emma barely bothered to remove her coat and hat before sweeping back down the grand staircase to direct the footman who was unloading her plants to place them in the hothouse. She followed him through a series of corridors until they emerged into the infamous structure, and she couldn't contain her gasp of delight.

"Oh, this is *perfect!*"

The footman placed her five precious orchids on a potting table by the doors, bowed, and left her to explore.

Emma gazed upwards. A dizzying cobweb of iron arches and struts rose overhead, supporting hundreds of panes of glass. The air was both hot and humid. Clouds of steam billowed from a metal grille in one corner, and when she dipped her fingers into one of the small raised pools that had been built between the enormous flower beds, the water was as hot as a bath.

Perfect.

"The heat comes from diverting naturally-hot water from a spring not far from here. As the Romans did, at Bath."

Emma spun around in surprise; she hadn't heard Kit enter the room. The sight of him made her pulse flutter erratically, but she sent him a friendly smile. "Ah, my lord. Good afternoon. I was just settling my plants into their new home."

"So I see."

"I've had my man of business write you a check," she said quickly. "I can go and—"

He waved his hand. "Later. I trust you."

He gestured for them to proceed down one of the pathways and Emma fell into step beside him, barely able to hide her delight at seeing so many familiar species of tropical plants thriving in the sultry conditions. Surely this boded well for her orchids.

"This place is wonderful! I've noted several plants I last saw back in Brazil."

"It was my father's pride and joy. But it's been sadly neglected these past few years."

While you were recovering from your imprisonment, Emma finished silently.

Her heart ached for all he had suffered. News of his convalescence had reached her, even in Brazil. She'd specifically asked after him in her letters home and her friend, Heloise Hampden—who happened to be married to Kit's good friend, William Ravenwood—had kept her abreast of his progress. It seemed he'd only recently returned to London life.

Should she be flattered that he'd broken his self-imposed exile to meet her at the docks?

No, she was reading too much into it. He was a man of his word. Of course he'd want to fulfill his promise to her brother.

"You have no interest in botany?" she asked.

He shrugged. "Some. I can certainly appreciate a pretty flower, but I'm nowhere near as passionate about the subject as you seem to be." He glanced back at her orchids. "I admit I find it hard to visualize anything blooming from such an unpromising tangle of roots."

Emma sent him a diffident look. "They *will* flower, now that they have adequate heat and light. This level of humidity is perfect, although I'm going to have to keep a close eye on them. Orchids are notoriously temperamental. Once the flowers appear, they will bloom for several weeks before the petals fall and they go back into a dormant stage again."

They'd stopped in front of a pool much larger than the rest. Unlike the others, the surface of this one was not covered in lilies and other water plants, and Emma spied a set of shallow stone steps leading down into it.

"Oh! A bathing pool!" she exclaimed in delight. "How wonderful!"

"Yes. The heat of the water is extremely effective in relaxing the body. Feel free to make use of it yourself. It is a wonderful feeling, to float about in the steam."

She smiled. "I can imagine. The way the mist hangs over the water reminds me of the early mornings on the Amazon. I never swam in that, of course. I was too afraid of crocodiles. But I would have liked to."

He swept his hand over the pool in a grand gesture. "Then consider this your invitation to gain another unique experience to add to your tally. I promise it's crocodile-free."

"Thank you."

He turned and started for the door, then swung back abruptly. "I'm afraid I cannot join you for dinner this evening, but I've asked Mrs. Bennington, my housekeeper, to serve you in your room. I wish you a pleasant evening."

Emma watched his retreat with a pang of regret. She would have liked to have dinner with him. His surly reticence intrigued her, although she could quite understand that it might stem from his mistreatment during the war.

But something about him called to her. She felt the most ridiculous urge to try to lighten his spirits, to draw him out of the protective shell he seemed to have built around himself. Her heart beat faster every time he glanced in her direction, and every time she made him smile it felt as if she'd conquered a mountain or forded a particularly challenging stream.

Lord, the man could prove dangerously addictive.

That evening, as she enjoyed toast and crumpets in her room by a crackling fire, Emma was taunted by the idea of him, swimming in that hot pool. What would his body look like? What did he wear to swim? Did he ever swim naked?

A flush that had nothing to do with the fire's heat engulfed her and she forced herself to think of other things. Cold things. Like whether it would snow tomorrow.

CHAPTER 5

*E*mma awoke to the unmistakable hush of snowfall and when she glanced out of the window of her room she almost squealed in excitement. Despite being almost twenty four, she retained a childlike fascination with the stuff—especially after the energy-sapping heat of South America.

Determined to take a brisk, invigorating walk in the gardens, she donned her stoutest boots, thick woolen stockings, and her warmest skirt. She'd just finished when a knock sounded at her door.

"Ah, Mrs. Bennington." She greeted the housekeeper with a warm smile. "Is that tea and toast I spy?"

"It is ma'am."

"You needn't have come all this way. I was about to come down."

"Oh, it's no bother, but I'm sorry we don't have a lady's maid to help you dress. Bess and Sarah have been given the week off to visit with their families, so we're a little short belowstairs."

"I quite understand. His lordship wasn't expecting visitors. Rest assured I'm quite capable of seeing to my own needs. Just pretend I'm not here."

The housekeeper returned her smile. "Yes ma'am."

As she scoffed down her breakfast, Emma mentally congratulated Kit on being a considerate employer. Many aristocratic houses entertained lavishly at this time of year, and the poor servants barely got a moment to themselves.

The formal gardens proved to be a delight, and she crunched happily through the snow, dodging low-hanging branches. A wilder patch of woodland grew a short distance past the maze, and she headed in that direction, her attention caught by the ball of greenery sprouting halfway along the branch of a sturdy oak tree. Since the oak's leaves had all fallen away, the puff of mistletoe was easy to spot.

She paused at the foot of the trunk and peered upward, her hands planted on her hips.

As someone who'd spent a great deal of time scampering around the rigging of her father's ships—her ships now, since the death of both her parents and Andrew—the branches of the stately oak provided little challenge.

Hiking her skirts, she began to climb. She'd just reached the limb where the mistletoe grew when a shout from below broke her concentration.

"What on earth do you think you're doing?"

Emma smiled. Kit was glaring up at her from the bottom of the tree.

"Dear God, woman, are you mad? You'll fall to your death!"

"I'm perfectly fine, but thank you," she called back cheerily. "And Merry Christmas. I'm just getting you a sprig of mistletoe for the house. I couldn't help noticing the lack of it in your festive decorations."

He winced at her sarcastic reference. Apart from a holly wreath on the front door, his 'festive decorations' were practically non-existent. She hid a grin. Teasing him was delightful.

"Andrew told me you were a genius at getting into scrapes," he growled. "I'm beginning to see what he meant."

Emma almost lost her footing on the branch. "You and Andrew talked about me?"

"Of course. We spent six months sharing a cell. We shared life stories."

She risked a glance down at him and was alarmed to see a roguish grin cross his face.

"He told me *all* your most embarrassing childhood tales."

Mortification brought a flush to her cheeks.

"I loved listening to them," he admitted. "I never had a sister. He loved you very much."

Her throat tightened with emotion, and she coughed to cover it, then busied herself snapping a handful of sprigs from the mistletoe. She started to descend, careful not to squash the sticky white berries against her skin.

"Mistletoe and orchids have something in common, you know," she called down. "They're both epiphytes."

"I have no idea what that means."

"Parasites," she laughed. "They both grow on another tree, getting moisture from the rain and feeding on the decomposing leaves of the host."

"Isn't that bad for the tree?"

"Not at all. They don't take anything, or harm it in any way."

"I hope, as *your* host, you're not going to harm me, either," he joked. "Or steal anything."

She snorted at his levity. "As if I could harm you. You're twice my size."

Unfortunately, she made the grave mistake of glancing down and became distracted by the impressive breadth of his shoulders and the twinkle in his eyes. As she reached for a snow-dusted branch, her fingers slipped, and she tumbled straight down toward him with a horrified yelp.

He lifted his arms to catch her, and the next thing she knew they were both sprawled on the ground beneath the tree in an ungainly tangle of limbs.

Oof!" he grunted.

Emma flushed scarlet and tried to push herself upright, but her skirts were rucked up around her knees and their legs were entwined as she straddled him. Her chest was plastered to his, and the hard muscles of his abdomen flexed beneath her palms as she slid them around for a place to push upright.

When she finally staggered to her feet she made a great show of brushing the snow from her skirts to hide her mortification. Kit rolled to his side and stood, chuckling as he, too, dusted the icy slush from his coat. He bent and retrieved the sprigs of mistletoe from where they lay strewn about and handed her the posy with a mocking bow.

"Your bouquet, madame."

Emma accepted it with a wry smile. "Thank you. I'm not usually so careless. The ice made it slicker than I expected."

He glanced up at the remaining ball of mistletoe growing directly above them and sent her a roguish grin. "That's the second time I've risked life and limb to save you from certain peril." He raised his brows in cheeky suggestion. "Why don't you honor tradition and reward me for my trouble?"

He tapped his cheek, indicating where she should kiss him.

Heat scalded up her neck and to the tops of her ears, but her heart pounded in appreciation of this new, flirtatious game. She'd dreamed of kissing Kit for years.

"Very well. Thank you for saving me. Again."

Balancing up on tiptoe, she pressed a chaste kiss to his cheek.

Her lips tingled. His skin was cool and slightly textured with early-morning beard, and her stomach somersaulted at the delicious scent of his cologne.

Just as she told herself to pull away, he turned his head, and the warm exhale of his breath sloughed over her lips. She froze, hardly daring to breathe. And then his lips brushed hers—a tentative, silent question—and Emma didn't think. She turned her own head and leaned up into him, fusing her mouth to his.

His low growl of satisfaction reverberated through her. His lips moved on hers, tasting, nibbling, even as his gloved hands came up to cup the back of her head.

Her knees almost gave out. *She was kissing Kit Carlisle!* And it was *glorious.*

When she parted her lips to suck in a breath he took full advantage; his tongue slipped inside and touched her own. Shocked but intrigued, Emma darted her own tongue out to brush against his, and the moment she did so the kiss turned wild. He kissed her again and again. Deep, languorous sweeps of his tongue, as if he couldn't get enough of her taste, as if he wished to consume her.

Enthralled, Emma grabbed the lapels of his coat and kissed him back with all the pent-up longing in her heart. A low, deep ache throbbed in her belly and between her legs.

Just when she thought she might faint from pleasure, he dragged his mouth from hers. His hands dropped from her nape and he took a cooling step backward.

"God, Emma, forgive me—"

"Don't you *dare* apologize," she scolded breathlessly.

He glanced down her in surprise. "I shouldn't have done that."

"No, I suppose not." She sent him a wry smile. "But I'm delighted you did."

The poor man looked as though she'd hit him over the head with an iron bar. Her smile widened even more.

"As first kisses go, it was lovely."

His jaw dropped open. "That was your first kiss?"

"It was," she admitted cheerfully. "At least, my first *proper* one. I had no idea people did that with their tongues."

He shook his head, still looking dazed. "But . . . how is that even possible? You're twenty-three for God's sake."

"I know how old I am. And it's entirely possible. I've hardly been in England since I was nineteen. You'd be amazed at the lack of potential suitors there are on the other side of the world."

"But—"

His gaze seemed fixated on her mouth, as if he was thinking of kissing her again, just for good measure. Emma rather hoped he would do just that, but to her disappointment he turned away and raked his hands distractedly through his hair.

"When Andrew asked me to *take care of you* I very much doubt that was what he meant," he growled.

Her heart contracted at the remorse and self-recrimination in his tone. "He asked that of you?"

"Yes."

She smiled, albeit a little sadly. "He always was the very best of brothers. But please don't imagine you have some sort of responsibility for me now. Andrew wouldn't have intended that at all. I'm sure he just meant for you to keep an eye out for me."

"Hmmm." Kit's growl was sufficient to convey his disagreement.

He started off toward the house, and it took her a long moment to catch up with him.

When she finally risked a glance at him, she deemed it prudent to ignore what had just happened, since he clearly seemed determined to forget it.

She rubbed her arm with a scowl. "I think I bruised my elbow."

"I think I bruised more than my elbow." He rubbed his backside. "I'm going to be black and blue by tomorrow."

Emma forced her eyes away from the sight of his large hand stroking his shapely posterior. The man had no right to look that good in breeches.

She cleared her throat as they neared the house. "I need to change and then check on my plants." She bobbed him a brief curtsey. "Good morning."

As much as she would have preferred to avoid Kit for the rest of the day, he was in the greenhouse when she finally made her way back downstairs. She went straight to her five remaining orchids and busied herself checking the dampness of their soil.

"What are you doing?" he asked.

She picked up a small jug from the potting table and scooped out a measure of warm water from the nearest pool. "They don't need watering until they're almost dried out. If they get too wet, they rot. That's why so many of them died on the way across the Atlantic—it was too damp for them on the ship."

"Ah."

Emma stroked a shiny leaf. "But this is a good sign that they're improving. See, how they've become a nice bright green? That means they're getting enough daylight. They were much darker when I first arrived."

Kit moved to stand at her shoulder and she tried not to bask in his nearness. Or think about what his lips had felt like on hers.

"I'm glad they're thriving in this environment," he said. "You seem to have a magic touch. Perhaps there's something about your presence that makes them want to live?"

She glanced sideways at him, unable to tell if he was serious or not. "I don't think there's any particular magic to it. I just care for them and give them what they need."

Do you *feel better in my presence?* She wanted to ask. *Do I make* you *want to live? To come alive?*

Where had those foolish thoughts come from?

* * *

KIT STARED at Emma's exquisite profile and swallowed down the admission that was forming on his tongue. How could he possibly explain that he felt like those orchids of hers? That he'd been in his own 'dormant stage' for the past eighteen months, but ... maybe she was coaxing him to bloom again?

His teasing suggestion that she kiss him under the mistletoe had been impulsive, a bit of fun, but the moment she'd stepped up close all he could think about was knowing the taste of her lips, the feel of her in his arms.

Kissing her had been a revelation.

She wasn't the first woman he'd been in contact with since his recovery, but she was the first one to truly rouse his interest—and his body. Desire, thick and dark, had pulsed through his bloodstream, reigniting passions he'd thought long dead.

He'd wanted to kiss her at sixteen when he'd visited her brother during their breaks from school. Now, at twenty five, he wanted to take her to bed and show her every pleasure that could be had between a man and a woman.

It wasn't only her physical body he craved, though. He admired her unflagging optimism and her thirst for life. Her vital presence had underscored how stagnant he'd allowed his own life to become, how drab and lacking in color.

He wanted to live again. Not merely to exist, but to expose himself to the world. To all the highs and lows it had to offer, despite the risks.

Two days in Emma's company, and he was dangerously close to declaring his undying love. He'd never seriously thought about his future before—it seemed like he'd be tempting fate to imagine it in prison—but now a whole vista of possibilities was opening up before him.

Getting married had seemed equally far-fetched. Despite the happy unions of his friends—Nic with Marianne, Raven with Heloise, and Richard with Sabine—he'd never really believed such a thing could happen to him. But Emma Townsend had turned his life upside down.

Andrew had been the very best of men, and his sister was cut from the same cloth. Caring, Kind. Fearless. The thought of being permanently attached to her wasn't so impossible to contemplate.

Kit snorted under his breath. The main flaw to that plan, of course, was that Emma was in no hurry to settle down. As a wealthy heiress with little interest in bowing to society's rules, she had the luxury of being able to go where she wished and do as she pleased.

She would be off on her next adventure as soon as she'd convinced the Botanical Society to acknowledge her latest discovery.

Still, he could enjoy her company for what little time they had together. Tomorrow was Christmas day and despite the fact that he'd been invited to spend the day with all three of his friends and their wives, he was glad he'd refused.

He would have Emma all to himself.

CHAPTER 6

*C*hristmas day dawned gray and chill, and a wicked idea seized Emma as she gazed out over the frost-hardened landscape. Her body ached in various places from her tumble from the tree, and as the cold seeped in between the leaded panes of the window the lure of a relaxing soak in the hot pool was too strong to ignore.

The house was barely staffed, and it was too early for Kit himself to be up and about.

She slipped into her dressing robe, grabbed a fresh bath linen from the rail, and descended the stairs. She knew the way to the hothouse now.

The place felt magical, like an exotic cathedral of green as she stepped through the double doors. Tendrils of steam swirled and skated over the surface of the water, playing in invisible currents. The air she sucked into her lungs was hot and wet; the droplets coated her throat and beaded her face like dew.

Condensation had made the hundreds of panes of glass opaque, adding a further sense of privacy. The scent of moist earth and fecund greenery stirred something within her, something base and primal, a connection to the earth and the incredible lush bounty it produced.

As she stepped to the edge of the bathing pool she debated whether to keep her cotton shift on for modesty, then decided against it. She wanted to know the decadent feel of the water completely unencumbered by clothing.

Discarding her shift, she started down the steps and a sigh of pure bliss escaped her as the heat of the water seeped into her body, from shins, to knees, to thighs. When she reached the last step the water was up to her waist and she sank down up to her shoulders with a groan of pleasure.

Oh, this was divine! If she ever decided to return to England permanently she would have to look into installing something just like this at her London residence. Or perhaps she should purchase a house somewhere here in Somerset? Near Kit.

Delighted with the thought, she cupped some water in her hands and let it trickle out along her arms, then lay back in the water and allowed herself to float. Her mind drifted to the sinful fantasy of Kit, there with her; the water lapping at her breasts and thighs were his hands, skimming over her in a sinful caress.

Her cheeks flushed even more.

After ten minutes of soaking, she regretfully left the water. It wouldn't do to be found swimming naked. She squeezed her hair and dried herself off, then donned her bathrobe and made her way back to her room.

THE MOMENT he heard the door close behind Emma Kit slumped back against the iron bench and let out a slow, calming exhale.

Dear God, he hadn't intended to spy on her bathing. He'd just been finishing up his daily round of exercises when she'd slipped in through the door. Since he'd been shirtless and sweaty he hadn't wanted to alarm her, so he'd ducked behind a clump of foliage, assuming she'd simply check on her precious plants and then leave.

Instead, however, he'd been frozen into immobility when she slid out of her dressing gown and tugged her chemise over her head.

The sight of her naked body had almost brought him to his knees. She was beautiful, like a golden goddess or mythical water nymph. A siren who could tempt a man gladly to his watery grave.

Watching her was so wrong. But even as Kit berated himself as the worst sort of scoundrel, he couldn't stop drinking her in. She was perfection. Smooth, rounded limbs, sweet breasts tipped with dusky pink nipples. Waist and hips so curved and inviting. He'd clenched his hands into fists against the need to touch. To see if her skin was as soft and luscious as it appeared.

When she'd slipped into the water and groaned her pleasure aloud he'd almost lost his mind. Droplets glistened over her shoulders and beaded on her cheeks and her skin had flushed a charming rosy shade from the heat. Kit had swallowed hard, praying for her to leave and end his torment . . . while simultaneously hoping the moment would never end.

After she finally left he felt his body relax once more. A wry smile stretched his lips. He couldn't have imagined a better Christmas present. Except for her naked in his bed.

CHAPTER 7

*L*ater that morning, Emma checked her plants and was delighted to see that at least two of the buds had opened into flowers. When Kit entered the greenhouse not long after, she greeted him with a euphoric smile.

"Look! They're starting to bloom! Come and see."

He crossed to her side and she tried to hide her blush. He really was the most handsome man. She forced herself to concentrate on the task at hand.

Each flower had five pointed outer petals, purple at the outer edges fading to almost white in the center. A darker amethyst 'trumpet' grew in the middle, the lower surface of which pouted like a lip. A trail of white, yellow, and orange led inside the flower's throat; an invitation for pollinating insects to come inside.

"I am certain this a new species," she said happily. "Part of the genus *oncidium*, except I've never heard of one with lavender petals like this, nor this frilled edge to the trumpet. I found them in northern Brazil, near Pernambuco, a thousand miles north of Rio de Janeiro."

Kit raised his brows. "I hope you're right. I've never been to South America, myself."

She slid him a sideways glance. "Have you never considered going?"

"It would be a great adventure. To be honest, after my imprisonment I never thought I'd want to go anywhere ever again, but you've reminded me that there's a whole world out there waiting to be explored. If only one has the courage."

Her heart swelled at the compliment. "Good. I'm glad." She sent him a cheeky smile. "You know, I'm always on the lookout for burly deckhands. Plus you know how to handle a weapon. Maybe you should consider a new career as an adventurer? Or as a personal bodyguard?"

Her heart pounded as he gazed down at her. Now that she'd voiced the idea aloud, she realized how much she liked it. How she would love to have Kit's company on one of her adventures. He was strong and surly, gruff and sweet, and despite his size and fierce demeanor he had an amazing ability to make her feel safe.

The intensity of his regard heated her cheeks and she looked away, suddenly self-conscious.

"I'll give it serious consideration," he said.

Flustered, Emma leaned over and sniffed at the nearest flower, then drew back in surprise. "Oh, it has a scent! I had no idea! Now I'm *sure* it's a new species. Orchids rarely have a perfume, but this one smells like roses."

Kit bent and inhaled near the second flower. "You're right."

"See, this is why I love orchids," Emma laughed happily. "They're like people. No two are exactly alike."

* * *

KIT GLANCED at the plant in front of him and then back over at Emma. The image of her, naked and rosy from the pool, overlaid his vision and he found himself transfixed by her eyes, her mouth. Her full lower lip had the same hint of a pout as that orchid of hers.

He grew hard.

She, however, was blithely unaware of his lascivious thoughts and sent him a friendly, open smile.

"Did you know that each type of orchid attracts its own particular pollinator? Some attract bees, while others need other types of insects. It means there's an enormous variety in appearance between different kinds."

Kit barely managed to grunt, and she carried on.

"I like to think that's true of people too. That everyone has some aspect of their character or appearance that will attract a specific person to them. That there's someone out there for everybody. An ideal match so to speak. We just have to find the right one."

She was looking up at him with such shining optimism that Kit felt a little dizzy. He had no idea where she was going with this conversation, but his heart was pounding. Was she suggesting that the two of *them* might be the perfect match for one another?

No, surely he was misinterpreting her words. Hearing things he wanted to hear.

He straightened up and bowed awkwardly, keeping his hands strategically in front of his crotch to hide the evidence of her nearness. "I'm going to see Mrs. Bennington about Christmas dinner. Excuse me."

CHAPTER 8

*D*espite the fact it was just the two of them for Christmas dinner, Emma had the most wonderful time. Fitzwilliam, the lone footman who'd helped unload her plants the day she'd arrived, seemed to be the only servant in attendance, but he kept her wineglass topped up and presented a dizzying array of courses prepared by Mrs. Bennington.

Perhaps it was the excellent burgundy loosening her tongue, but conversation flowed easily between herself and Kit as they shared tales of their adventures. He described some amusing incidents he'd had in Spain before he and Andrew had been captured, while Emma made him smile by recounting the time a monkey had invaded her cabin, opened her clothes chest, and stolen one of her favorite hats.

By the time a flaming Christmas pudding was placed on the table between them, with the warmed brandy flames flickering blue and orange, she decided it was time to reveal her final problem. Kit gave her the perfect opening.

"So, now that you've successfully managed to coax flowers from your plants, I assume you're ready to return to London and present them to the gentlemen of the Botanical Society?"

Emma toyed with her glass, suddenly nervous. "Well, as to that, there is one *small* matter in which I still need your help."

His brows rose.

"The Society is expecting one D. Townsend to present to them."

"And?"

Emma decided to come clean. "They think the D stands for David."

Kit put down his glass with a thump. "They think you're a *man?*"

"I'm afraid so. But you have to understand that it was the only way I could get them to take me seriously. They don't allow women to become members. And so every time I sent them a report from the field, with my drawings and notes, I used the fictitious name of David Townsend."

Kit's face was impassive. "David was your brother's middle name."

"Yes. It was."

He pinched his nose between his brows. "So they think this chap, David Townsend, is coming to present these new orchids at their meeting next week. What are you going to do?"

Emma sent him her most winning smile. "I was rather hoping I could persuade *you* to present them for me."

"Don't be ridiculous! I might not have been much in society for the past couple of years, but there are scores of people who'll recognize me. I've played cards with half the men who make up the Botanical Society. I can't masquerade as a botanist named Townsend."

Emma reached over and touched his sleeve. "I'm not asking you to pretend to be anyone except yourself. You can just say you're David Townsend's benefactor, and that he's been taken ill. We can make up some tropical disease or something. He'll be too ill to attend, so he's entrusted you with presenting his discovery."

"You want me to lie," he said flatly.

She rushed to explain, hating the disapproval in his tone. "A tiny little white lie for an excellent cause. Even if you don't care about the advancement of science, do it for Andrew. It'll allow his name to go down in history, immortalized in a plant."

He opened his mouth, but Emma cut him off, determined to sway him.

"You think I like it?" she growled. "I don't. It's monstrously unfair. I've done all of the work, but I'll never receive any credit. The only thing I can do is to ensure that my surname—the one shared with my brother—gets linked to these plants." She lifted her chin and gave him a direct stare. "That will have to be enough."

"You're sure women aren't allowed to join the society?"

"I've read the rules, and while they do not *specifically* preclude women from becoming a fellow, I have little doubt that my appearance would be seen in a very negative light. I don't want my gender to be the reason my discovery isn't accepted."

She sighed, and her anger dissipated into something closer to weary resignation. "They've had no problem with the papers I sent them for the past year. They're just too bull-headed to acknowledge that a woman might actually be their equal in terms or intellect and scientific ability."

Kit was quiet for a long moment, and Emma risked another glance up at him. "If I can accept that I must hide my achievements behind a fictional name, then surely you can stand up and speak to a bunch of your peers for ten minutes or so."

He took a deep drink of his wine, and she waited for his answer with bated breath.

"It's not an unreasonable request," he said slowly, as if choosing his words with care. "It's just that ever since my imprisonment I've disliked large crowds of people. I would find it very uncomfortable to be the center of attention at somewhere like the Botanical Society."

Oh.

His unexpected admission stole the wind from her sails. Only a strong man could admit a weakness, even to himself. It required even more strength to disclose it to a woman.

His honesty was utterly endearing. *Damn it.* She didn't want to force him to relive any painful experience. But who else could she ask?

"Lord Wellington once said he had two rules for public speaking," Kit continued. "One: never take on subjects you know nothing about and, two; whenever possible, avoid quoting Latin. You're asking me to do both those things."

"Not the Latin—"

He lifted his brows. "I listened to my father go on about plants long enough to know that they all have long, unpronounceable Latin names. What's the name you want for your new flower? Something long-winded, I'll bet."

Emma wrinkled her nose in an effort not to laugh at his accurate guess. "Well, yes. I want it to be called *Oncidium Townsendiae Purpurea.* But that only means purple Townsend oncidium. It's very simple to say, really." She sent him another pleading look across the table.

"I don't know the first thing about orchids."

"I'll help you. I'll give you detailed notes and tell you everything you need to say. You can do it Kit. Help me. Please."

His sigh came from the very depths of his soul. "Oh, all right."

Emma clapped her hands as triumph filled her. "Yes! Thank you! That's the best Christmas present I could possibly have wished for."

For some reason her comment brought an embarrassed flush to his cheeks and he took a rapid gulp of wine but Emma was too delighted at his agreement to ponder why.

"The society's next meeting is three days away. There's plenty of time for you to practice what you have to say before we go back up to London."

CHAPTER 9

*E*mma made her way through the quiet house with a deep sense of wistfulness. She would miss her early-morning dips when she returned to London tomorrow. She'd become very fond of everything at Ashford court.

Including its owner.

She and Kit had spent several hours going over the speech he would give to the Botanical Society. Despite his misgivings she was confident that he would acquit himself admirably.

Yesterday afternoon he'd taken her on a tour of the grounds, showing her the places he'd toured with Andrew when her brother had visited. The two of them had shared countless bitter-sweet reminiscences along with a laugh or two over some of the more humorous memories.

Since the lake had frozen over, they'd even gone ice-skating. Emma had thrilled every time Kit had taken her hand, or grabbed her waist to steady her. She'd secretly hoped he'd kiss her again, and although an undeniable tension rippled between them, he maintained a gentlemanly distance.

He probably thought of their mistletoe kiss as a mistake, but

Emma knew that she would cherish it as one of her fondest memories.

When she reached the conservatory she slipped through the glass door. Anticipation coursed through her veins as she imagined the wonderful sensation of hot water against her skin. The room was so steamy it was impossible to see from one end to the other, and an unexpected splash of water sent her scurrying behind the nearest shrub.

Someone had beaten her to it!

Her heart began to pound. Was it *Kit?*

Tiptoeing forward for a better view, she peered through the leafy green fronds. Her breath caught in her throat as Kit emerged from the rippling water, and her eyes grew wide as his head, shoulders, and back slowly appeared.

Dear God, he was magnificent. Like Triton or Poseidon.

The muscles of his upper arms flexed as he pushed his wet hair back from his face, and Emma bit her lip at the breadth of his shoulders and the way his ribs tapered down to a trim waist. The water, most unhelpfully, ended there; she got a tantalizing peek at the indents at the base of his spine and the merest glimpse of taut, round buttocks when he moved.

She let out a slow, measured breath.

Then he turned.

Oh, Lord. Heat flashed over her skin.

Water sluiced over his collarbones and down the perfectly sculpted planes of his chest. His abdomen was ridged in a way that made her fingers itch to trace each perfect undulation. An intriguing line of dark hair arrowed southwards from his navel and disappeared below the waterline, teasing her with what she couldn't see.

Emma's mouth went dry. Although she'd seen countless shirtless sailors and dock hands on her travels, she'd never seen a fully naked man before. Based on what she *had* seen, none of them compared to Kit.

Heloise had said Kit had been close to starvation when Raven had rescued him from Spain, but there was no sign of such deprivation now. He was a man in his prime, glorious to behold.

She wanted to see more.

He sank back into the water and swam lazily over to the opposite end of the pool. When he ducked back under the water, Emma saw her chance. The pile of his discarded clothing—shirt and breeches—lay just within reach, on one of the low stone walls. Before he could resurface, she darted forward, grabbed them, and dived back behind her palm.

She had to bite her lip to stifle her cackle of delight. She'd played this same trick on Andrew countless times when they'd been children, swimming in the lake. Kit needed a little teasing in his life. He was far too serious.

Five minutes later, and her patience was rewarded. Kit rose from the pool and slowly ascended the steps. Streams of water sluiced off him, lovingly caressing his skin. Even thought she could only see him from behind, her laughter died. The whole of his body was revealed, from rounded buttocks, strong thighs and slim, muscled calves.

And then he leaned and caught up a bath sheet she hadn't noticed from the side, and she pouted in frustration. He dried himself, unhurried, and Emma sighed when he wrapped the linen around his waist and secured it at the front, hiding his glorious backside from view.

She saw the exact moment he realized his clothes were gone. He peered this way and that, then bent over and searched along the floor, as if expecting them to have fallen down somewhere.

A snort of laughter, completely unbidden, escaped her mouth. She clapped her hand over her lips, but it was too late. Kit froze, but instead of whirling round to confront her, he placed his hands slowly on his hips.

"I do believe a naughty little garden sprite has been in here and stolen my clothes," he growled.

His tone was a thrilling combination of threat and amusement and Emma barely suppressed another laugh.

"I wonder where she could be?"

He finally turned, giving her another marvelous view of his chest and hair-darkened legs protruding below the sheet. Emma prayed the fabric's knot would fail, so she might glimpse the part of his anatomy that was causing the intriguing bulge between his legs, but the fabric seemed damnably secure.

Disappointing.

Kit stalked in her direction. She ducked lower, her stomach twisting in mingled dread and excitement. He was almost upon her, about to discover her hiding place, when she let out a squeal and leapt to her feet.

"Aha!" He lunged forward with a roar and made a grab for her nightgown, but she was too quick. She tossed his shirt and breeches at him, hitting him squarely in the face, and used his momentary blindness to dart past him.

"You little wretch!"

She dashed for the entrance with a strangled shriek.

As she reached the door, she realized he wasn't in hot pursuit. Out of breath from both the sight of his nakedness and the sprint, she stopped and turned, one hand on the door handle. She found him shaking his head with a reluctant smile on his handsome face.

"Andrew said you were always playing tricks on him. I see you haven't lost the talent."

Her cheeks were flaming, but Emma send him a cheeky curtsey. "Why, thank you. I aim to please."

A muscle twitched in his jaw and his knuckles whitened on his shirt. His hot gaze swept her from head to toe and Emma's skin tingled in response.

"Oh, you please me, Miss Townsend," he murmured. "You please me very much."

Emma didn't know what to say. Part of her wanted to step

back across the room, to throw herself against his still-damp body, and demand that he kiss her again. She almost countered with, "Do *you* want to please *me*?" but she didn't have the nerve.

She was playing with fire, taunting him like this. She could get hurt so easily if she wasn't careful. But oh, how she wanted to burn.

An awkward silence descended until he cleared his throat and turned away. "Ahem. I assume you came down here to bathe? If you'll give me five minutes, I'll get out of your way."

Emma nodded. "Yes. Of course."

She didn't see him for the rest of the day, much to her disappointment.

CHAPTER 10

As Kit stared out at the countless faces in the raked auditorium, all of them regarding him with varying degrees of confusion, expectation, and surprise, he felt a trickle of sweat snake down the back of his collar.

He shuffled the copious hand-written notes Emma had given him, and glanced over at the purple flowers bobbing merrily on the table set up just to the right of his lectern. Two of the five plants that had been in his hothouse had failed to flower, but the remaining three were causing a ripple of delighted speculation throughout the room.

He lifted his chin and found Emma in the crowd. She'd taken a seat directly in front of the lectern, in his line of vision, and the sight of her calmed the thunderous pounding of his heart.

He took a breath and willed his clammy palms to stop sweating. *He could do this.* These men were his peers, not enemy combatants who wished him harm. This well-lit lecture hall was a world away from the airless cell he'd endured with Andrew in Spain.

The reminder of his friend strengthened Kit's resolve. Just as he'd been determined to return Emma's locket to her, so *she* was determined to name these plants after her brother. Kit could make that happen. He wouldn't let his fear of public speaking, nor the overwhelming number of people in the room, stop him.

Emma had been allowed to accompany him as his guest, and he'd been amused to see the speculative looks the two of them had received from the other men. No doubt news of their joint outing would reach the ears of the society wives by this evening.

The thought of Emma's name tied to his own didn't dismay him in the least, but since she was no simpering debutante and was known to be a law unto herself when it came to playing by society's rules, he didn't think anyone would expect them to marry because of the scandal.

He almost wished they would.

He caught her eye again and an immense calm settled over him. The rest of the room blurred as he stared at her; the beautiful green of her eyes, those perfect, kissable lips.

He would pretend she was the only person in the room, that he was speaking only to her. They were back at Ashford Court, in the hothouse, not in this draughty auditorium full of stuffy old men.

His heartrate slowed and his breathing deepened as he relaxed. He concentrated on remembering her scent, the smooth plane of her cheek, the breathtaking beauty of her naked form as she swam in the pool at dawn.

He cleared his throat, and his voice was calm and steady.

"*Lady* and Gentlemen." He sent her a smile which she returned with a delighted nod of acknowledgment for the courtesy. "I am here before you today on behalf of a good friend of mine, Mister David Townsend. It grieves me to report than Mr. Townsend himself is unable to be with us today for the unveiling of what, I'm sure you will agree, is a momentous new addition to the genus *Orchidaceae.*" He swept his arm toward the flowering plants to his right. "I present to you, *Oncidium Townsendiae Purpurea.*"

* * *

"YOU DID IT!"

Emma laughed breathlessly as they both sank back in his carriage. "Oh, I knew you could! Thank you!"

Kit smiled at her from his seat on the opposite swab. "I'm just glad I managed to present your case well enough that they agreed to adopt the new name. And to acknowledge your entirely new sub-species."

He sent a wry glance at the orchids, their purple flowers bobbing merrily from the crate on the floor. Emma put her fingers to her throat and touched the small silver locket that hung there, suspended from a new thin chain.

"I think Andrew brought us luck."

"Yes. He'd have been very proud."

Emma's heart was full to overflowing. With pride, for the fact that she'd finally honored Andrew's memory with something lasting and meaningful. With gratitude to the man opposite her, for overcoming his natural reticence to champion her cause. And with a poignant sadness that their time together was coming to an end.

She didn't want it to end. She'd enjoyed his company far too much this past week.

"What do you say to a celebratory glass of port at my town-house, Lady Townsend?"

"I'd like that," she smiled.

A sense of reckless urgency seized her.

Her ship, the Medusa, was in the process of being refitted and restocked. She would be leaving on another plant-hunting trip to Brazil in less than two weeks. But why shouldn't she grasp this brief moment of happiness with Kit? She was twenty three and she'd never had a lover, and until she'd reencountered him she'd really not considered herself missing anything. But her body reacted to him in the most extraordinary ways and she was consumed by curiosity to know what it would be like to abandon all propriety and touch that incredible body of his without restraint.

To have him touch her in return.

She didn't expect him to marry her, of course. But perhaps, as long as they took the necessary precautions to avoid pregnancy, they could share a week of passion before she sailed for the other side of the world.

Her stomach somersaulted at the thought. The carriage rocked to a stop, and she clasped Kit's hand as he helped her descend the steps and led her into the entrance of his townhouse.

Suddenly self-conscious—because, really, how did one suggest to a man that you wished to become his lover?—she allowed the austere butler to take her cloak then followed Kit into what appeared to be a study.

She accepted the glass of wine he poured from the sideboard and smiled when he tapped the rim of his own glass against hers.

"A toast," he said. "To a successful joint venture."

"And to new *adventures*," she quipped.

They studied each other as they sipped their drinks.

"I have something to ask you—"

"I have a confession to make—"

They both laughed as they spoke at the same time.

"I'm sorry, you go first," Emma said quickly. "What's your confession?"

Kit's grey eyes were steady on her own. "It's rather scandalous, I'm afraid."

She raised her eyebrows. "Well, if you must know, so is the thing I wish to ask you."

He lifted his own brows in unabashed interest, but she gestured at him with her glass. "But I insist you go first."

"Very well. I saw you bathing in the hot pool, back at Ashford court. On Christmas morning."

Heat scalded her cheeks. "You did?"

"I'm afraid so."

His expression appeared grave, but there was a twinkle in his eyes and the ghost of a smile at the corner of his mouth. Her heart began to pound.

"You saw me naked?"

"Unintentionally. You walked in just as I'd finished my morning exercises. I didn't want to alarm you, so I ducked behind a plant. I had no idea you planned to swim. By the time I realized that was your intent, you'd already stripped off."

Emma was sure her cheeks were crimson, but she forced herself to hold his intense gaze. "And . . . did you like what you saw?"

"I did. You're exquisite, Emma Townsend."

It was now or never. Time to seize the moment.

"Would you like to see me naked again?"

She held her breath, and time seemed to stop as she waited for his reply.

"I would like that very much." His voice was hoarse, almost a whisper. "But you're about to leave on another adventure. You haven't time for a trip back to Somerset and a dip in my pool."

Excitement and terror swirled low in her belly. "Perhaps we could . . . try it without a pool?"

With slow deliberation he set down his glass, then took hers and placed it next to his own. Her pulse fluttered as his fingers brushed hers. Kit stepped closer and lifted his hand to cup her cheek. "Are you suggesting we have an affair?"

"I believe I am."

He shook his head. "Well, in that case, I'm sorry, but I can't accept."

Her spirits plummeted. How could she have misread him so

completely? God, she was such a fool! She opened her mouth to try to salvage the situation, but he wrapped his free arm around her waist and drew her forward when she would have pulled away.

"No!" he said gruffly. "Let me finish. Please."

She stilled.

"I don't want a brief affair. I want more."

"But I'm not staying in England," she said. "I have plans. There's a whole world out there to discover."

"I don't want you to leave." He frowned and shook his head as if frustrated with his own inarticulacy. "No, that's not true. I *do* want you to leave because that's what makes you happy, and I'd never stop you doing what you love."

"But—"

"What I mean is, I don't want you to leave me behind." His grey eyes bored into hers as he let out a long, unsteady breath. "I used to like being alone. Preferred it, even. But I'll be lonely without you. Lonely and thoroughly miserable."

Emma could hardly believe her ears. Her heart was pounding so fast she was sure he would be able to hear it.

His arm tightened around her waist. "What if I . . . came with you?"

The hesitancy in his voice was as surprising as it was endearing.

She frowned. "You mean as my bodyguard? As a member of my crew?" Elation filled her as the idea took shape. "I don't see why not. Every expedition needs a good, strong porter to—"

He shook his head. "Not as a porter. At least, not only as that, although I'll carry your plants whenever you want me to. I was thinking more along the lines of . . . husband."

Her mouth dropped open. "Husband?"

He smiled at her shock and used his thumb to gently stroke her jaw. "Yes, if you'll have me. I want to be a part of all your adventures. I want to *live*, not merely exist."

"But . . . the jungles of Brazil are teeming with dangerous creatures and unwelcoming—"

"—and I can't wait to discover them all with you." He gave a rueful shrug. "I know I don't have much in the way of fortune, and I'm a grumpy devil at the best of times, but I *do* have a very impressive hothouse. And if that doesn't sway you, then I think you should know that . . . I love you beyond measure."

She gasped, and he let out a wry chuckle. "I think I've loved you from the moment you fell out of that tree and flattened me. Maybe even before that. Before I even went off to war. I never stopped thinking of you, even when I was in prison. I prayed that I'd live, so I could come back and find you again."

His gaze bored into hers. "I believe Andrew knew, or at least suspected. I think, in asking me to give you that locket, he was . . . giving us his blessing. But it doesn't matter what he would have wanted. What matters is what *you* want." He traced her lips with his fingertip. "Do you want me, Emma? Will you marry me?"

Emma didn't have to think twice. Of all the men she'd ever met, she couldn't imagine anyone better at her side. She threw her arms around his neck.

"Well, it would be rather scandalous if we just sailed off together *without* getting married," she conceded breathlessly. "But that's not why I'm saying yes. I'm saying yes because I love you too."

His broad shoulders slumped in relief, and a devilish twinkle kindled in his eye.

"In that case, I take back what I said about having an affair. It will take a few days to get a Special License from the Archbishop of Canterbury, and I can't go another hour without taking you to bed. Shall we be lovers until we're officially wed?"

Emma's stomach flipped with excitement. "Oh, yes please!" Her cheeks heated in anticipation, even as she sent him a cheeky glance. "I'd like to see *you* naked. It's only fair."

He laughed outright, and the deep rumble warmed her right

through. "You got bloody close, stealing my clothes when I was bathing," he scolded.

She tried and failed to look remorseful. "I kept hoping that bath sheet would unwind, but you must tie incredibly tight knots. It was most disappointing."

His grey eyes twinkled with roguish intent. "That's not what you'll be saying *after* we've made love, I promise you."

She lifted herself up on tiptoe, offering herself up for a kiss, and Kit needed no further encouragement. He took her mouth in a kiss that left her breathless; fierce and tender at once. His big hands came up to cradle the back of her head, and she almost swooned in delight as his tongue swept inside to tangle with her own.

They were both panting when he finally dragged his mouth from hers.

"Come upstairs?" he growled.

Emma nodded, utterly certain. "Yes."

A giggle escaped her as he caught her behind the knees and swept her up into his arms. He strode to the door, crossed the hallway, and mounted the stairs two at a time.

She wound her arms around his neck and rained kisses along the side of his jaw, savoring his groan of impatience and the heady scent of his skin. He was overwhelming in the best possible way, but she had no doubt that he would be a considerate lover. He'd known pain and loss, just as she had, but his heart was both loyal and true.

She couldn't wait to start the next chapter of her life with him at her side. It was going to be another marvelous adventure. . .

THE END.

WANT TO READ MORE? You can get a FREE novella, Kate's Egypt-set romp The Promise of a Kiss, when you sign up to her newsletter: https://www.kcbateman.com/subscribe/

AND READ on for a sneak peek of This Earl Of Mine, the first book in Kate's Bow Street Bachelors series . . .

*R*ead on for a sneak peek of *This Earl Of Mine,* the first exhilarating historical romance in Kate Bateman's Bow Street Bachelors Series. . .

This Earl Of Mine

Chapter 1.
London, March 1816.

There were worse places to find a husband than Newgate Prison.

Of course there were.

It was just that, at present, Georgie couldn't think of any.

"Georgiana Caversteed, this is a terrible idea."

Georgie frowned at her burly companion, Pieter Smit, as the nondescript carriage he'd summoned to convey them to London's most notorious jail rocked to a halt on the cobbled street. The salt-weathered Dutchman always used her full name whenever he disapproved of something she was doing. Which was often.

"Your father would turn in his watery grave if he knew what you were about."

That was undoubtedly true. Until three days ago, enlisting a husband from amongst the ranks of London's most dangerous criminals had not featured prominently on her list of life goals. But desperate times called for desperate measures. Or, in this case, for a desperate felon about to be hanged. A felon she would marry before the night was through.

Georgie peered out into the rain-drizzled street, then up, up the near-windowless walls. They rose into the mist, five stories high, a vast expanse of brickwork, bleak and unpromising. A church bell tolled somewhere in the darkness, a forlorn clang like a death knell. Her stomach knotted with a grim sense of foreboding.

Was she really going to go through with this? It had seemed a good plan, in the safety of Grosvenor Square. The perfect way to thwart Cousin Josiah once and for all. She stepped from the carriage, ducked her head against the rain, and followed Pieter under a vast arched gate. Her heart hammered at the audacity of what she planned.

They'd taken the same route as condemned prisoners on the way to Tyburn tree, only in reverse. West to east, from the rarefied social strata of Mayfair through gradually rougher and bleaker neighborhoods, Holborn and St. Giles, to this miserable place where the dregs of humanity had been incarcerated. Georgie felt as if she were nearing her own execution.

She shook off the pervasive aura of doom and straightened her spine. This was her choice. However unpalatable the next few minutes might be, the alternative was far worse. Better a temporary marriage to a murderous, unwashed criminal than a lifetime of misery with Josiah.

They crossed the deserted outer courtyard, and Georgie cleared her throat, trying not to inhale the foul-smelling air that seeped from the very pores of the building. "You have it all arranged? They are expecting us?"

Pieter nodded. "Aye. I've greased the wheels with yer blunt, my girl. The proctor and the ordinary are both bent as copper shillings. Used to having their palms greased, those two, the greedy bastards."

Her father's right-hand man had never minced words in front of her, and Georgie appreciated his bluntness. So few people in the ton ever said what they really meant. Pieter's honesty was refreshing. He'd been her father's man for twenty years before she'd even been born. A case of mumps had prevented him from accompanying William Caversteed on his last, fateful voyage, and Georgie had often thought that if Pieter had been with her father, maybe he'd still be alive. Little things like squalls, shipwrecks, and attacks from Barbary pirates would be mere inconveniences to a man like Pieter Smit.

In the five years since Papa's death, Pieter's steadfast loyalty had been dedicated to William's daughters, and Georgie loved the gruff, hulking manservant like a second father. He would see her through this madcap scheme—even if he disapproved.

She tugged the hood of her cloak down to stave off the drizzle. This place was filled with murderers, highwaymen, forgers, and thieves. Poor wretches slated to die, or those "lucky" few whose sentences had been commuted to transportation. Yet in her own way, she was equally desperate.

"You are sure that this man is to be hanged tomorrow?"

Pieter nodded grimly as he rapped on a wooden door. "I am. A low sort he is, by all accounts."

She shouldn't ask, didn't want to know too much about the man whose name she was purchasing. A man whose death would spell her own freedom. She would be wed and widowed within twenty-four hours.

Taking advantage of a condemned man left a sour taste in her mouth, a sense of guilt that her happiness should come from the misfortune of another. But this man would die whether she married him or not. "What are his crimes?"

"Numerous, I'm told. He's a coiner." At her frown, Pieter elaborated. "Someone who forges coins. It's treason, that."

"Oh." That seemed a little harsh. She couldn't imagine what that was like, having no money, forced to make your own. Still, having a fortune was almost as much of a curse as having nothing. She'd endured six years of insincere, lecherous fortune hunters, thanks to her bountiful coffers.

"A smuggler too," Pieter added for good measure. "Stabbed a customs man down in Kent."

She was simply making the best out of a bad situation. This man would surely realize that while there was no hope for himself, at least he could leave this world having provided for whatever family he left behind. Everyone had parents, or siblings, or lovers. Everyone had a price. She, of all people, knew that—she was buying herself a husband. At least this way there was no pretense. Besides, what was the point in having a fortune if you couldn't use it to make yourself happy?

Pieter hammered impatiently on the door again.

"I know you disapprove," Georgie muttered. "But Father would never have wanted me to marry a man who covets my purse more than my person. If you hadn't rescued me the other evening, that's precisely what would have happened. I would have had to wed Josiah to prevent a scandal. I refuse to give control of my life and my fortune to some idiot to mismanage. As a widow, I will be free."

Pieter gave an eloquent sniff.

"You think me heartless," Georgie said. "But can you think of another way?" At his frowning silence, she nodded. "No, me neither."

Heavy footsteps and the jangle of keys finally heralded proof of human life inside. The door scraped open, and the low glare of a lantern illuminated a grotesquely large man in the doorway.

"Mr. Knollys?"

The man gave a brown-toothed grin as he recognized Pieter. "Welcome back, sir. Welcome back." He craned his neck and raised the lantern, trying to catch a glimpse of Georgie. "You brought the lady, then?" His piggy eyes narrowed with curiosity within the folds of his flabby face.

"And the license." Pieter tapped the pocket of his coat.

Knollys nodded and stepped back, allowing them entry. "The ordinary's agreed to perform the service." He turned and began shuffling down the narrow corridor, lantern raised. "Only one small problem." He cocked his head back toward Pieter. "That cove the lady was to marry? Cheated the 'angman, 'e 'as."

Pieter stopped abruptly, and Georgie bumped into his broad back.

"He's dead?" Pieter exclaimed. "Then why are we here? You can damn well return that purse I paid you!"

The man's belly undulated grotesquely as he laughed. It was not a kindly sound. "Now, now. Don't you worry yerself none, me fine lad. That special license don't have no names on it yet, do it? No. We've plenty more like 'im in this place. This way."

The foul stench of the prison increased tenfold as they followed the unpleasant Knollys up some stairs and down a second corridor. Rows of thick wooden doors, each with a square metal hatch and a sliding shutter at eye level lined the walls on either side. Noises emanated from some—inhuman moans, shouts, and foul curses. Others were ominously silent. Georgie pressed her handkerchief to her nose, glad she'd doused it in lavender water.

Knollys waddled to a stop in front of the final door in the row. His eyes glistened with a disquieting amount of glee.

"Found the lady a substitute, I 'ave." He thumped the metal grate with his meaty fist and eyed Georgie's cloaked form with a knowing, suggestive leer that made her feel as though she'd been drenched in cooking fat. She resisted the urge to shudder.

"Wake up, lads!" he bellowed. "There's a lady 'ere needs yer services."

Chapter 2.

Benedict William Henry Wylde, scapegrace second son of the late Earl of Morcott, reluctant war hero, and former scourge of the ton, strained to hear the last words of his cellmate. He bent forward, trying to ignore the stench of the man's blackened teeth and the sickly sweet scent of impending death that wreathed his feverish form.

Silas had been sick for days, courtesy of a festering stab wound in his thigh. The bastard jailers hadn't heeded his pleas for water, bandages, or laudanum. Ben had been trying to decipher the smuggler's ranting for hours. Delirium had loosened the man's tongue, and he'd leaned close, waiting for something useful to slip between those cracked lips, but the words had been frustratingly fragmented. Silas raved about plots and treasons. An Irishman. The emperor. Benedict had been on the verge of shaking the poor bastard when his crewmate let out one last, gasping breath—and died.

"Oh, bloody hell!"

Ben drew back from the hard, straw-filled pallet that stank of piss and death. He'd been so close to getting the information he needed.

Not for the first time, he cursed his friend Alex's uncle, Sir Nathaniel Conant, Chief Magistrate of Bow Street and the man tasked with transforming the way London was policed. Bow Street was the senior magistrate court in the capital, and the "Runners," as they were rather contemptuously known, investigated crimes, followed up leads, served warrants and summons, searched properties for stolen goods, and watched premises where infringements of bylaws or other offences were suspected.

Conant had approached Ben, Alex, and their friend Seb about a year ago, a few months after their return from fighting Napoleon on the continent. The three of them had just opened the Tricorn Club—the gambling hell they'd pledged to run together while crouched around a smoky campfire in Belgium. Conant had pointed out that their new venture placed them in an ideal position for gathering intelligence on behalf of His Majesty's government, since its members—and their acquaintances—came from all levels of society. He'd also requested their assistance on occasional cases, especially those which bridged the social divide. The three of them not only had entrée into polite society, but thanks to their time in the Rifles, they dealt equally well with those from the lower end of the social spectrum, the "scum of the earth," as Wellington had famously called his own troops.

Conant paid the three of them a modest sum for every mission they undertook, plus extra commission for each bit of new information they brought in. Neither Alex nor Seb needed the money; they were more interested in the challenge to their wits, but Benedict had jumped at the chance of some additional income, even though the work was sometimes—such as now— less than glamorous.

He was in Newgate on Conant's orders, chasing a rumor that someone had been trying to assemble a crew of smugglers to rescue the deposed Emperor Napoleon from the island of St. Helena. Benedict had been ingratiating himself with this band for weeks, posing as a bitter ex-navy gunner, searching for the man behind such a plan. He'd even allowed himself to be seized by customs officials near Gravesend along with half the gang— recently deceased Silas amongst them—in the hopes of discovering more. If he solved this case, he'd receive a reward of five hundred pounds, which could go some way toward helping his brother pay off the mass of debt left by their profligate father.

He'd been in here almost ten days now. The gang's ringleader, a vicious bastard named Hammond, had been hanged yesterday morning. Ben, Silas, and two of the younger gang members had been sentenced to transportation. That was British leniency for you; a nice slow death on a prison ship instead of a quick drop from Tyburn tree.

The prison hulk would be leaving at dawn, but Ben wouldn't be on it. There was no need to hang around now that Silas and Hammond were both dead. He'd get nothing more from them. And the two youngsters, Peters and Fry, were barely in their teens. They knew nothing useful. Conant had arranged for him to "disappear" from the prison hulk before it sailed; its guards were as open to bribery as Knollys.

Several other gang members had escaped the Gravesend raid. Benedict had glimpsed a few familiar faces in the crowd when the magistrate had passed down his sentence. He'd have to chase them down as soon as he was free and see if any of them had been approached for the traitorous mission.

Benedict sighed and slid down the wall until he sat on the filthy floor, his knees bent in front of him. He'd forgotten what it felt like to be clean. He rasped one hand over his stubbled jaw and grimaced—he'd let his beard grow out as a partial disguise. He'd commit murder for a wash and a razor. Even during the worst scrapes in the Peninsular War, and then in France and Belgium, he'd always found time to shave. Alex and Seb, his brothers-in-arms, had mocked him for it mercilessly.

He glanced at the square of rain visible through the tiny barred grate on the outer wall of his cell. Seb and Alex were out there, lucky buggers, playing merry hell with the debutantes, wives, and widows of London with amazing impartiality.

The things he did for king and bloody country.

And cash, of course. Five hundred pounds was nothing to sneeze at.

Tracking down a traitor was admirable. Having to stay celibate and sober because there was neither a woman nor grog to be had in prison was hell. What he wouldn't give for some decent French brandy and a warm, willing wench. Hell, right now he'd settle for some of that watered-down ratafia they served at society balls and a tumble with a barmaid.

A pretty barmaid, of course. His face had always allowed him to be choosy. At least, it did when he was clean-shaven. His own mother probably wouldn't recognize him right now.

Voices and footsteps intruded on his errant fancies as the obsequious voice of Knollys echoed through the stones. A fist slammed into the grate, loud enough to wake the dead, and Benedict glanced over at Silas with morbid humor. Well, almost loud enough.

"Wake up, lads!" Knollys bellowed. "There's a lady 'ere needs yer services."

Benedict's brows rose in the darkness. What the devil?

"Ye promised ten pounds if I'd find 'er a man an' never say nuffink to nobody," he heard Knollys say through the door.

"Are they waiting to hang too?" An older man's voice, that, with a foreign inflexion. Dutch, perhaps.

"Nay. Ain't got no more for the gallows. Not since Hammond yesterday." Knollys sounded almost apologetic. "But either one of these'll fit the bill. Off to Van Diemen's Land they are, at first light."

"No, that won't do at all."

Benedict's ears pricked up at the sound of the cultured female voice. She sounded extremely peeved.

"I specifically wanted a condemned man, Mr. Knollys."

"Better come back in a week or so then, milady."

There was a short pause as the two visitors apparently conferred, too low for him to hear.

"I cannot wait another few weeks." The woman sounded resigned. "Very well. Let's see what you have."

Keys grated in the lock and Knollys's quivering belly filled the doorway. Benedict shielded his eyes from the lantern's glare, blinding after the semidarkness of the cell. The glow illuminated Silas's still figure on the bed and Knollys grunted.

"Dead, is 'e?" He sounded neither dismayed nor surprised. "Figured he wouldn't last the week. You'll 'ave to do then, Wylde. Get up."

Benedict pushed himself to his feet with a wince.

"Ain't married, are you, Wylde?" Knollys muttered, low enough not to be heard by those in the corridor.

"Never met the right woman," Benedict drawled, being careful to retain the rough accent of an east coast smuggler he'd adopted. "Still, one lives in 'ope."

Knollys frowned, trying to decide whether Ben was being sarcastic. As usual, he got it wrong. "This lady's 'ere to wed," he grunted finally, gesturing vaguely behind him.

Benedict squinted. Two shapes hovered just outside, partly shielded by the jailer's immense bulk. One of them, the smaller hooded figure, might possibly be female. "What woman comes here to marry?"

Knollys chuckled. "A desperate one, Mr. Wylde."

The avaricious glint in Knollys's eye hinted that he saw the opportunity to take advantage, and Benedict experienced a rush of both anger and protectiveness for the foolish woman, whoever she might be. Probably one of the muslin set, seeking a name for her unborn child. Or some common trollop, hoping her debts would be wiped off with the death of her husband. Except he'd never met a tart who spoke with such a clipped, aristocratic accent.

"You want me to marry some woman I've never met?" Benedict almost laughed in disbelief. "I appreciate the offer, Mr.

Knollys, but I'll have to decline. I ain't stepping into the parson's mousetrap for no one."

Knollys took a menacing step forward. "Oh, you'll do it, Wylde, or I'll have Ennis bash your skull in." He glanced over at Silas's corpse. "I can just as easy 'ave 'im dig two graves instead of one."

Ennis was a short, troll-like thug who possessed fewer brains than a sack of potatoes, but he took a malicious and creative pleasure in administering beatings with his heavy wooden cudgel. Benedict's temper rose. He didn't like being threatened. If it weren't for the manacles binding his hands, he'd explain that pertinent fact to Mr. Knollys in no uncertain terms.

Unfortunately, Knollys wasn't a man to take chances. He prodded Benedict with his stick. "Out with ye. And no funny business." His meaty fist cuffed Ben around the head to underscore the point.

Benedict stepped out into the dim passageway and took an appreciative breath. The air was slightly less rancid out here. Of course, it was all a matter of degree.

A broad, grizzled man of around sixty moved to stand protectively in front of the woman, arms crossed and bushy brows lowered. Benedict leaned sideways and tried to make out her features, but the hood of a domino shielded her face. She made a delicious, feminine rustle of silk as she stepped back, though. No rough worsted and cotton for this lady. Interesting.

Knollys prodded him along the passage, and Benedict shook his head to dispel a sense of unreality. Here he was, unshaven, unwashed, less than six hours from freedom, and apparently about to be wed to a perfect stranger. It seemed like yet another cruel joke by fate.

He'd never imagined himself marrying. Not after the disastrous example of his own parents' union. His mother had endured his father's company only long enough to produce the requisite heir and a spare, then removed herself to the gaiety of London. For the next twenty years, she'd entertained a series of lovers in the town house, while his father had remained immured in Herefordshire with a succession of steadily younger live-in mistresses, one of whom had taken it upon herself to introduce a seventeen-year-old Benedict to the mysteries of the female form. It was a pattern of domesticity Benedict had absolutely no desire to repeat.

In truth, he hadn't thought he'd survive the war and live to the ripe old age of twenty-eight. If he had ever been forced to picture his own wedding—under torture, perhaps—he was fairly certain he wouldn't have imagined it taking place in prison. At the very least, he would have had his family and a couple of friends in attendance; his fellow sworn bachelors, Alex and Seb. Some flowers, maybe. A country church.

He'd never envisaged the lady. If three years of warfare had taught him anything, it was that life was too short to tie himself to one woman for the rest of his life. Marriage would be an imprisonment worse than his cell here in Newgate.

They clattered down the stairs and into the tiny chapel where the ordinary, Horace Cotton, was waiting, red-faced and unctuous. Cotton relished his role of resident chaplain; he enjoyed haranguing soon-to-be-dead prisoners with lengthy sermons full of fire and brimstone. No doubt he was being paid handsomely for this evening's work.

Benedict halted in front of the altar—little more than a table covered in a white cloth and two candles—and raised his manacled wrists to Knollys. The jailer sniffed but clearly realized he'd have to unchain him if they were to proceed. He gave Ben a sour, warning look as the irons slipped off, just daring him to try something. Ben shot him a cocky, challenging sneer in return.

How to put a stop to this farce? He had no cash to bribe his way out. A chronic lack of funds was precisely why he'd been working for Bow Street since his return from France, chasing thief-taker's rewards.

Could he write the wrong name on the register, to invalidate the marriage? Probably not. Both Knollys and Cotton knew him as Ben Wylde. Ex-Rifle brigade, penniless, cynical veteran of Waterloo. It wasn't his full name, of course, but it would probably be enough to satisfy the law.

Announcing that his brother happened to be the Earl of Morcott would certainly make matters interesting, but thanks to their father's profligacy, the estate was mortgaged to the hilt. John had even less money than Benedict.

The unpleasant sensation that he'd been neatly backed into a corner made Benedict's neck prickle, as if a French sniper had him in his sights. Still, he'd survived worse. He was a master at getting out of scrapes. Even if he was forced to marry this mystery harridan, there were always alternatives. An annulment, for one.

"Might I at least have the name of the lady to whom I'm about to be joined in holy matrimony?" he drawled.

The manservant scowled at the ironic edge to his tone, but the woman laid a silencing hand on his arm and stepped around him.

"You can indeed, sir." In one smooth movement, she pulled the hood from her head and faced him squarely. "My name is Georgiana Caversteed."

Benedict cursed in every language he knew.

Chapter 3.

Georgiana Caversteed? What devil's trick was this?

He knew the name, but he'd never seen the face—until now. God's teeth, every man in London knew the name. The chit was so rich, she might as well have her own bank. She could have her pick of any man in England. What in God's name was she doing in Newgate looking for a husband?

Benedict barely remembered not to bow—an automatic response to being introduced to a lady of quality—and racked his brains to recall what he knew of her family. A cit's daughter. Her father had been in shipping, a merchant, rich as Croesus. He'd died and left the family a fortune.

The younger sister was said to be the beauty of the family, but she must indeed be goddess, because Georgiana Caversteed was strikingly lovely. Her arresting, heart-shaped face held a small straight nose and eyes which, in the candlelight, appeared to be dark grey, the color of wet slate. Her brows were full, her lashes long, and her mouth was soft and a fraction too wide.

A swift heat spread throughout his body, and his heart began to pound.

She regarded him steadily as he made his assessment, neither dipping her head nor coyly fluttering her lashes. Benedict's interest kicked up a notch at her directness, and a twitch in his breeches reminded him with unpleasantly bad timing of his enforced abstinence. This was neither the time nor the place to do anything about that.

They'd never met in the ton. She must have come to town after he'd left for the peninsula three years ago, which would make her around twenty-four. Most women would be considered on the shelf at that age, unmarried after so many social seasons, but with the near-irresistible lure of her fortune and with those dazzling looks, Georgiana Caversteed could be eighty-four and someone would still want her.

And yet here she was.

Benedict kept his expression bland, even as he tried to breathe normally. What on earth had made her take such drastic action? Was the chit daft in the head? He couldn't imagine any situation desperate enough to warrant getting leg-shackled to a man like him.

She moistened her lips with the tip of her tongue—which sent another shot of heat straight to his gut—and fixed him with an imperious glare. "What is your name, sir?" She took a step closer, almost in challenge, in defiance of his unchained hands and undoubtedly menacing demeanor.

He quelled a spurt of admiration for her courage, even if it was ill-advised. His inhaled breath caught a subtle whiff of her perfume. It made his knees weak. He'd forgotten the intoxicating scent of woman and skin. For one foolish moment, he imagined pulling her close and pressing his nose into her hair, just filling his lungs with the divine scent of her. He wanted to drink in her smell. He wanted to see if those lips really were as soft as they looked.

He took an involuntary step toward her but stopped at the low growl of warning from her manservant. Sanity prevailed, and he just remembered to stay in the role of rough smuggler they all expected of him.

"My name? Ben Wylde. At your service."

His voice was a deep rasp, rough from lack of use, and Georgie's stomach did an odd little flip. She needed to take command here, like Father on board one of his ships, but the man facing her was huge, hairy, and thoroughly intimidating.

When she'd glanced around Knollys's rotund form and into the gloomy cell, her first impression of the prisoner had been astonishment at his sheer size. He'd seemed to fill the entire space, all broad shoulders, wide chest, and long legs. She'd been expecting some poor, ragged, cowering scrap of humanity. Not this strapping, unapologetically male creature.

She'd studied his shaggy, overlong hair and splendid proportions from the back as they'd traipsed down the corridor. He stood a good head taller than Knollys, and unlike the jailer's waddling shuffle, this man walked with a long, confident stride, straight-backed and chin high, as if he owned the prison and were simply taking a tour for his pleasure.

Now, in the chapel, she finally saw his face—the parts that weren't covered with a dark bristle of beard—and her skin prickled as she allowed her eyes to rove over him. She pretended she was inspecting a horse or a piece of furniture. Something large and impersonal.

His dark hair was matted and hung around his face almost to his chin. It was hard to tell what color it would be when it was clean. A small wisp of straw stuck out from one side, just above his ear, and she resisted a bizarre feminine urge to reach up and remove it. Dark beard hid the shape of his jaw, but the candlelight caught his slanted cheekbones and cast shadows in the hollows beneath. The skin that she could see—a straight slash of nose, cheeks, and forehead—was unfashionably tanned and emphasized his deep brown eyes.

She'd stepped as close to him as she dared; no doubt he'd smell like a cesspool if she got any nearer, but even so, she was aware of an uncomfortable curl of . . . what? Reluctant attraction? Repelled fascination?

The top of her head only came up to his chin, and his size was, paradoxically, both threatening and reassuring. He was large enough to lean on; she was certain if she raised her hand to his chest, he would be solid and warm. Unmovable. Her heart hammered in alarm. He was huge and unwashed, and yet her body reacted to him in the most disconcerting manner.

His stare was uncomfortably intense. She dropped her eyes, breaking the odd frisson between them, and took a small step backward.

His lawn shirt, open at the neck, was so thin it was almost transparent. His muscled chest and arms were clearly visible through the grimy fabric. His breeches were a nondescript brown, snug at the seams, and delineated the hard ridges of muscles of his lean thighs with unnerving clarity.

Georgie frowned. This was a man in the prime of life. It seemed wrong that he'd been caged like an animal. He exuded such a piratical air of command that she could easily imagine him on the prow of a ship or pacing in front of a group of soldiers, snapping orders.

She found her voice. "Were you in the military, Mr. Wylde?"

That would certainly explain his splendid physique and air of cocky confidence.

His dark brows twitched in what might have been surprise but could equally have been irritation. "I was."

She waited for more, but he did not elaborate. Clearly Mr. Wylde was a man of few words. His story was probably like that of thousands of other soldiers who had returned from the wars and found themselves unable to find honest work. She'd seen them in the streets, ragged and begging. It was England's disgrace that men who'd fought so heroically for their country had been reduced to pursuing a life of crime to survive.

Was the fact that he was not a condemned man truly a problem? Her original plan had been to tell Josiah she'd married a sailor who had put to sea. She would have been a widow, of course, but Josiah would never have known that. Her "absent" husband could have sailed the world indefinitely.

If she married this Wylde fellow, she would not immediately become a widow, but the intended result would be the same. Josiah would not be able to force her into marriage and risk committing bigamy.

Georgie narrowed her eyes at the prisoner. They would be bound together until one or the other of them died, and he looked disconcertingly healthy. Providing he didn't take up heavy drinking or catch a nasty tropical disease, he'd probably outlive her. That could cause problems.

Of course, if he continued his ill-advised occupation, then he'd probably succumb to a knife or a bullet sooner rather than later. Men like him always came to a sticky end; he'd only narrowly escaped the gallows this time. She'd probably be a widow in truth soon enough. But how would she hear of his passing if he were halfway across the world? How would she know when she was free?

She tore her eyes away from the rogue's surprisingly tempting lips and fixed Knollys with a hard stare. "Is there really no one else? I mean, he's so . . . so . . ."

Words failed her. Intimidating? Manly?

Unmanageable.

"No, ma'am. But he won't bother you after tonight."

What alternative did she have? She couldn't wait another few weeks. Her near-miss with Josiah had been the last straw. She'd been lucky to escape with an awful, sloppy kiss and not complete ruination. She sighed. "He'll have to do. Pieter, will you explain the terms of the agreement?"

Pieter nodded. "You'll marry Miss Caversteed tonight, Mr. Wylde. In exchange, you'll receive five hundred pounds to do with as you will."

Georgie waited for the prisoner to look suitably impressed. He did not. One dark eyebrow rose slightly, and the corner of his mobile lips curled in a most irritating way.

"Fat lot of good it'll do me in here," he drawled. "Ain't got time to pop to a bank between now and when they chain me to that floating death trap in the morning."

He had a fair point. "Is there someone else to whom we could send the money?"

His lips twitched again as if at some private joke. "Aye. Send it to Mr. Wolff at number ten St. James's. The Tricorn Club. Compliments of Ben Wylde. He'll appreciate it."

Georgie had no idea who this Mr. Wolff was—probably someone to whom this wretch owed a gambling debt—but she nodded and beckoned Pieter over. He took his cue and unfolded the legal document she'd had drawn up. He flattened it on the table next to the ordinary's pen and ink.

"You must sign this, Mr. Wylde. Ye can read?" he added as an afterthought.

Another twitch of those lips. "As if I'd been educated at Cambridge, sir. But give me the highlights."

"It says you renounce all claim to the lady's fortune, except for the five hundred pounds already agreed. You will make no further financial demands upon her in the future."

"Sounds reasonable."

The prisoner made a show of studying the entire document, or at least pretending to read it, then dipped the pen into the ink. Georgie held her breath.

Papa's will had divided his property equally between his wife and two daughters. To Georgie's mother, he'd left the estate in Lincolnshire. To her sister, Juliet, he'd left the London town house. And to Georgie, his eldest, the one who'd learned the business at his knee, he'd left the fleet of ships with which he'd made his fortune, the warehouses full of spices and silk, and the company ledgers.

His trusted man of business, Edmund Shaw, had done an exemplary job as Georgie's financial guardian for the past few years, but in three weeks' time, she would turn twenty-five and come into full possession of her fortune. And according to English law, as soon as she married, all that would instantly become the property of her husband, to do with as he wished.

That husband would not be Josiah.

Despite her mother's protests that it was vulgar and unladylike to concern herself with commerce, in the past five years Georgie had purchased two new ships and almost doubled her profits. She loved the challenge of running her own business, the independence. She was damned if she'd give it over to some blithering idiot like Josiah to drink and gamble away.

Which was precisely why she'd had Edmund draw up this detailed document. It stated that all property and capital that was hers before the marriage remained hers. Her husband would receive only a discretionary allowance. To date, she'd received seven offers of marriage, and each time she'd sent her suitor to see Mr. Shaw. Every one of them had balked at signing—proof, if she'd needed it, that they'd only been after her fortune.

She let out a relieved sigh as the prisoner's pen moved confidently over the paper. Ben Wylde's signature was surprisingly neat. Perhaps he'd been a secretary, or written dispatches in the army? She shook her head. It wasn't her job to wonder about him. He was a means to an end, that was all.

He straightened, and his brown eyes were filled with a twinkle of devilry. "There, now. Just one further question, before we get to the vows, Miss Caversteed. Just what do you intend for a wedding night?"

Want to read more? Check out This Earl Of Mine on your favorite retailer.

ABOUT THE AUTHOR

Kate Bateman, also writing as K.C. Bateman, is a #1 bestselling author of Regency and Renaissance historical romances, including *The Secrets & Spies* series, the *Bow Street Bachelors* series, and the *Ruthless Rivals series*. Her Renaissance romp, *The Devil To Pay* was a 2019 RITA award finalist.

She's also an auctioneer and fine art appraiser, the co-founder and director of Bateman's Auctioneers, a fine art and antiques auction house in the UK. She currently lives in Illinois with her husband and three inexhaustible children, but returns to England regularly to appear as an antiques expert on several popular BBC television shows.

Kate loves to hear from readers. Contact her via her website: www.kcbateman.com and sign up for her newsletter to receive regular updates on new releases, giveaways and exclusive excerpts.

Follow Kate online for the latest new releases, giveaways, exclusive sneak peeks, and more!

Join Kate's Facebook reader group: Badasses in Bodices

Sign up for Kate's monthly-ish newsletter via her website for news, exclusive excerpts and giveaways.

Follow Kate Bateman on Bookbub for new releases and sales.
Add Kate's books to your Goodreads lists, or leave a review!

Follow:

Facebook: https://www.facebook.com/kcbatemanauthor/
Twitter: http://twitter.com/katebateman
Instagram: https://www.instagram.com/kc_bateman/
Join Kate's FB reader Group 'Badasses In Bodices': http://
bit.ly/JoinKatesBadasses

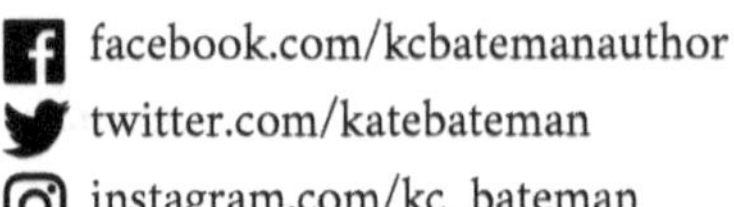

www.ingramcontent.com/pod-product-compliance
Lightning Source LLC
Chambersburg PA
CBHW021749190726
48290CB00008B/2548